MARGRET & H.A. REY'S

Curious George

Feeds the Animals

Illustrated in the style of H. A. Rey by Vipah Interactive

Houghton Mifflin Harcourt
Boston   New York

Copyright © 1998 by Houghton Mifflin Harcourt Publishing Company

Based on the character of Curious George®, created by Margret and H. A. Rey.
Illustrated by Vipah Interactive, Wellesley, Massachusetts: C. Becker, D. Fakkel, M. Jensen,
S. SanGiacomo, C. Witte, C. Yu.

www.hmhbooks.com

The text of this book is set in 17 point Adobe Garamond.
The illustrations are watercolor and charcoal pencil, reproduced in full color.

Library of Congress Cataloging-in-Publication Data

Curious George feeds the animals / based on the original character by Margret and
H. A. Rey.
p.   cm.
Summary: Curious George gets in trouble by feeding the animals at the zoo, but when a
parrot escapes from the rainforest exhibit he is able to save the day.
ISBN 978-0-547-54785-5
[1. Monkeys — Fiction. 2. Zoos — Fiction. 3. Parrots — Fiction.] I. Rey, Margret,
1906–1996. II. Rey, H. A. (Hans Augusto), 1898–1977. III. Vipah Interactive.
PZ7.C921364   1998
[Fic] — dc21   98-21327
                                                       CIP AC

Manufactured in China
LEO 10 9 8 7 6 5 4 3 2 1
4500276614

This is George.

George was a good little monkey and always very curious.

One day George went to the zoo with his friend, the man with the yellow hat. A new rain forest exhibit was opening and they wanted to be the first ones inside.

But when they got to the new exhibit, the doors were closed. "We'll have to come back later, George," the man said. "Why don't we visit the other animals while we wait?"

First they stopped to watch a zookeeper feed the seals. When he tossed little fish in the air, the seals jumped up to catch them. Then they barked for more.

It looked like fun to feed the animals!

"Would you like something to eat, too, George?" asked the man with the yellow hat, and he bought a snack for them to share.

When they stopped to see the crocodile, George remembered how the zookeeper had fed fish to the seals. He was curious. Would the crocodile like something to eat?

George tossed him a treat—and the crocodile snapped it out of the air!

Next they visited the koalas. George thought the koalas were cute. Here was a friendly one — she was curious, too. She wanted to see what George was eating, so he held out his hand to share.

George shared his treats with an elephant

and a baby kangaroo.

George was making lots
of new friends at the zoo.
The lion was already eating, but
the hippopotamus tried a snack.
Next he gave a treat to an ostrich.

11

Then George saw the giraffes. What fun to feed a giraffe! Giraffes usually have their heads up high in the trees, but George could see these giraffes would be easy to feed.

But as soon as he held out his hand, a zookeeper came running. The zookeeper looked angry. Was he angry with George? George didn't know — and he didn't want to stay to find out. He slipped away...

and the giraffes were happy to help!

But where did George go?

He was trying his best to hide. But little monkeys can't stay still for long. When George wiggled, the zookeeper was waiting. "I see you!" he said.

Just then another zookeeper hurried by. "Come quick!" she yelled. "Someone saw the parrot!"

The first zookeeper led George to a bench.

"The parrot from our new exhibit escaped and I must help find it," he explained.

He told George to wait for him there, and before he left he said, "Don't you know you're not supposed to feed the animals? The wrong food might make them sick."

George felt awful.

He didn't know he wasn't supposed to feed the animals. He didn't want to make them sick.

George was looking at the treat in his hand when all of a sudden,

a big bird swooped
down and snatched it right up!
Now George knew he wasn't supposed to
feed the animals... but this one had helped itself.

A zookeeper passing by was happy to see George. "You found the parrot!" she said. "We've been looking for this bird all day."

When she saw George's snack, she said, "This isn't the best thing to feed a parrot, but a little won't hurt. Would you like to help me put him back where he belongs?"

George was glad to help after all the trouble he had caused, and together they went back to the exhibit.

RAIN FOREST

"There's our problem," the zookeeper said, pointing to a hole in the netting. As the zookeepers discussed how to fix it, George had an idea....

He climbed up like only a monkey can, and when he reached the hole — he tied the netting back together!

Meanwhile, the first zookeeper returned. "Catch that naughty monkey!" he yelled. "He was feeding the animals!"

"But that little monkey found the parrot," another zookeeper told him. "And look — he fixed the netting. Now we can open the exhibit."

When George came down, all the zookeepers cheered.

Finally the celebration began and the doors were opened. The man with the yellow hat was there, and he and George got to be the first ones inside!

As George walked in, the zookeepers thanked him for all his help. "Please visit anytime!" they said.

George couldn't wait to come back and see his friends. But next time he'd remember, unless you're a zookeeper...

24